Angelina at the Palace

Story by **Katharine Holabird** Illustrations by **Helen Craig**

PUFFIN

ngelina could hardly believe her furry ears when Miss Lilly invited her on a special visit to the Royal Palace of Mouseland.

"I'm helping the princesses prepare a dance for Queen Seraphina and King Ferdinand's wedding anniversary," Miss Lilly explained. "Will you be my helper?"

"Oh, yes please," cried Angelina, and she was so excited she did three perfect pirouettes.

"Can I come too?" begged Cousin Henry. Angelina shook her head, but Henry promised to be good, so Miss Lilly said he could come.

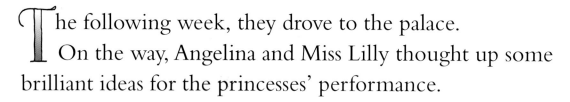

The following week, they drove to the palace.
On the way, Angelina and Miss Lilly thought up some brilliant ideas for the princesses' performance.

"Look!" squeaked Henry as the royal flags came into view.

Angelina and Henry marvelled at all the tall
towers and admired the handsome guards
in their gleaming armour.

That evening, Queen Seraphina invited her guests to a grand dinner. Angelina couldn't believe how beautiful the three princesses were with their sparkling jewels, flowing gowns and perfect table manners.

Angelina tried hard to be perfect, just like them. But the more she worried, the clumsier she became, until finally, she spilled soup all over her best dress!

*A*fterwards, Angelina was so upset, she sat on her big bed and hugged Mousie.

"I wish I was as graceful as the princesses," she sobbed.
"In the morning, I'll tell Miss Lilly that I want to go home.
I'm not good enough to be her helper."

Angelina snuggled under the covers. "Thank goodness you're here, Mousie," she sighed, drifting off to sleep.

But the next morning when Angelina went to knock on Miss Lilly's door, there was no answer.

"Miss Lilly!" cried Angelina, peeping round the door. "Are you all right?"

"I've caught a terrible cold," said Miss Lilly with a sneeze. "Could you teach the princesses for me?"

Angelina was horrified, but she knew she couldn't let Miss Lilly down.

"I'll do my best," Angelina promised, "but please get better soon."

Then she ran to
find Henry to explain
what had happened.

"You're my helper now!" she told him, and
they raced off together to the Grand Ballroom.

Shouts and shrieks were coming from the ballroom, and Angelina was astonished to see the princesses fighting.

"I want to be the magic fairy!" shouted Princess Valentina, pinching Sophie's ears.

"No – *I* want to be the magic fairy!" screamed Princess Sophie, pulling Valentina's whiskers.

"That's not fair – what about me?" howled little Princess Phoebe, yanking her sisters' tails.

Angelina suddenly realized that the princesses weren't so perfect after all.

Angelina clapped her paws for attention, just like Miss Lilly.

"I know a ballet with lots of magic fairies," she said. The princesses were so impressed that they stopped fighting to listen.

"Does it have a dragon?" asked Sophie.

"And a fairy island?" asked Phoebe.

"And a brave knight?" squeaked Henry.

"Definitely," said Angelina, starting
to feel less wobbly. "I'll show you."

After that, the princesses rehearsed with Angelina and Henry every day, while the royal seamstresses sewed sparkling fairy costumes and the royal carpenters built a magical stage set and a very fierce dragon.

Angelina was the Queen of the Fairies. She showed the princesses how to dance together and leap away from the dragon, and fly to safety on Fairy Island. The princesses loved dancing like fairies, and Henry was so proud to be the brave knight, he wanted his costume to be perfect.

Finally it was time for the big performance.
The king and queen and all their guests gathered in the Grand Ballroom to watch the show. Luckily Miss Lilly was well enough to come, even though she still had the sniffles.

Backstage, the princesses had butterflies in their tummies.

"What if we forget our steps?" worried Sophie.

"Don't worry," Angelina said kindly. "I know you'll be brilliant. Now, on with the show!"

A trumpet blew and Angelina twirled onstage, leading her band of fairies.

The princesses remembered everything they'd learned and they performed the *Fairy Island* ballet just like real ballerinas.

They leaped and pirouetted beautifully together, and not one of them tripped up or forgot her part.

When the dragon roared, the little fairies flew quickly across the stage
and waited for their brave knight to appear.

Oh dear, thought Angelina, *where is Henry?*

Just then she heard CLANK! CLANK! CLANK! and a muffled squeak, and Henry marched onstage in a real suit of armour, waving a *real* sword!

At the end of the show, Angelina invited Miss Lilly to come onstage. The audience stood and clapped as the performers took a final bow.

"Hip hip hooray! Three cheers for Angelina!" cried the princesses.

The End